Abney and Teal, how does it feel,

To live in the park on an island?

It's just right for us – it's adventurous!

And it's home, home on our island.

First published 2012 by Walker Books Ltd
87 Vauxhall Walk, London SE11 5HJ

10 9 8 7 6 5 4 3 2

Text by Stella Gurney
Illustrations by Joel Stewart

The Adventures of Abney & Teal © & ™
2011 Ragdoll Worldwide Ltd. Produced by Ragdoll.
Licensed by BBC WW Ltd. BBC logo ™ & © BBC 1996.

This book has been typeset in AbneyandTeal font

Printed in China

British Library Cataloguing in Publication Data: a catalogue record
for this book is available from the British Library

ISBN 978-1-4063-4490-5

www.walker.co.uk

The Adventures of
ABNEY & TEAL
Brilliant Boots

Joel Stewart

WALKER BOOKS
AND SUBSIDIARIES
LONDON • BOSTON • SYDNEY • AUCKLAND

It's a bright and shiny day on the island,
just right for something to happen.
Abney and Teal are enjoying the sunshine.
Across the water, Toby Dog plays an enjoying-
the-sunshine tune, and the Poc-Pocs are dancing.

bounce
twirl

"Hello, Bop!" waves Teal. "I like your new hat!"

"I don't think it's a hat, Teal," says Abney.

"I know what it is!"

"It's a **Something**," says Teal.

Bop takes the
Something off his
head and peers at it.

Then he takes a sip from it, instead
of from his stripy blue teacup.

What a **magnificent** bubble!

Bop tries another sip from
the Something, but - oh dear -
all the water has leaked out.
It doesn't make a very good
cup after all.

"Well!" says Teal. "It's Something,
but it's not a hat, and it's not a cup.
What else could we use it for?"
It looks like the Poc-Pocs have an idea.
Careful, Poc-Pocs!

cheep

cheep

chirrup

whee!

Whoops!

Too late! Down they tumble,
inside the Something.

poc

poc poc

whizz

whirl

Neep pops up and tips the **Something** over so the Poc-Pocs can hop out.

Neep!

poc poc-poc!

"**So** it's not a hat," says Teal, "and it's not a cup, and it's not a slide." "I know what it is!" says Abney.

Neep
Neep!

vroom vroom!

Neep jumps inside the **Something** and
begins to vroom about, just like it's a car.

"It could be a car, Neep!"
says Abney. "But I think
this **Something** is a boot,
to go on your foot.

Look!"

"Oh," says Abney, falling over. "This boot is
not very good. And there's only one."
"Never mind," cries Teal.
"We'll find some more boots!"

So they all have a look-about
for some better boots.

Abney and Teal go to see what they can find on Abney's shelves.

"Hmmm. I've got some string and some springs."

"Yippee, string!" cries Teal.

"Ooh," says Abney. "I've got an idea!"

"Me too!" says Teal.

boing-boing

boing

Wahoo!

The Poc-Pocs are excited. Oh, look!
They have found little acorn cups
for boots. They fit perfectly.

poc
poc-poc!

"Look at me, Teal!" calls Abney.
"I've found some lovely blue striped boots."

"Oh, Abney,"
claps Teal.
"They're **beautiful!**"

"They're a bit tricky
to walk in!"
says Abney.

Whoa!

"Oopsie. Oh, Teal –
I think I'm going to –

Whoops!

...fall over!"

Teal giggles. "Perhaps we should just use
your bowls for porridge, Abney?"
"I think you might be right, Teal,"
chuckles Abney.

So Abney makes a big pot of porridge for everyone.

poc-poc

Neep!

chirrup

"That was an adventure, wasn't it, Abney?"
sighs Teal, happily.
"Yes," agrees Abney. "It was."

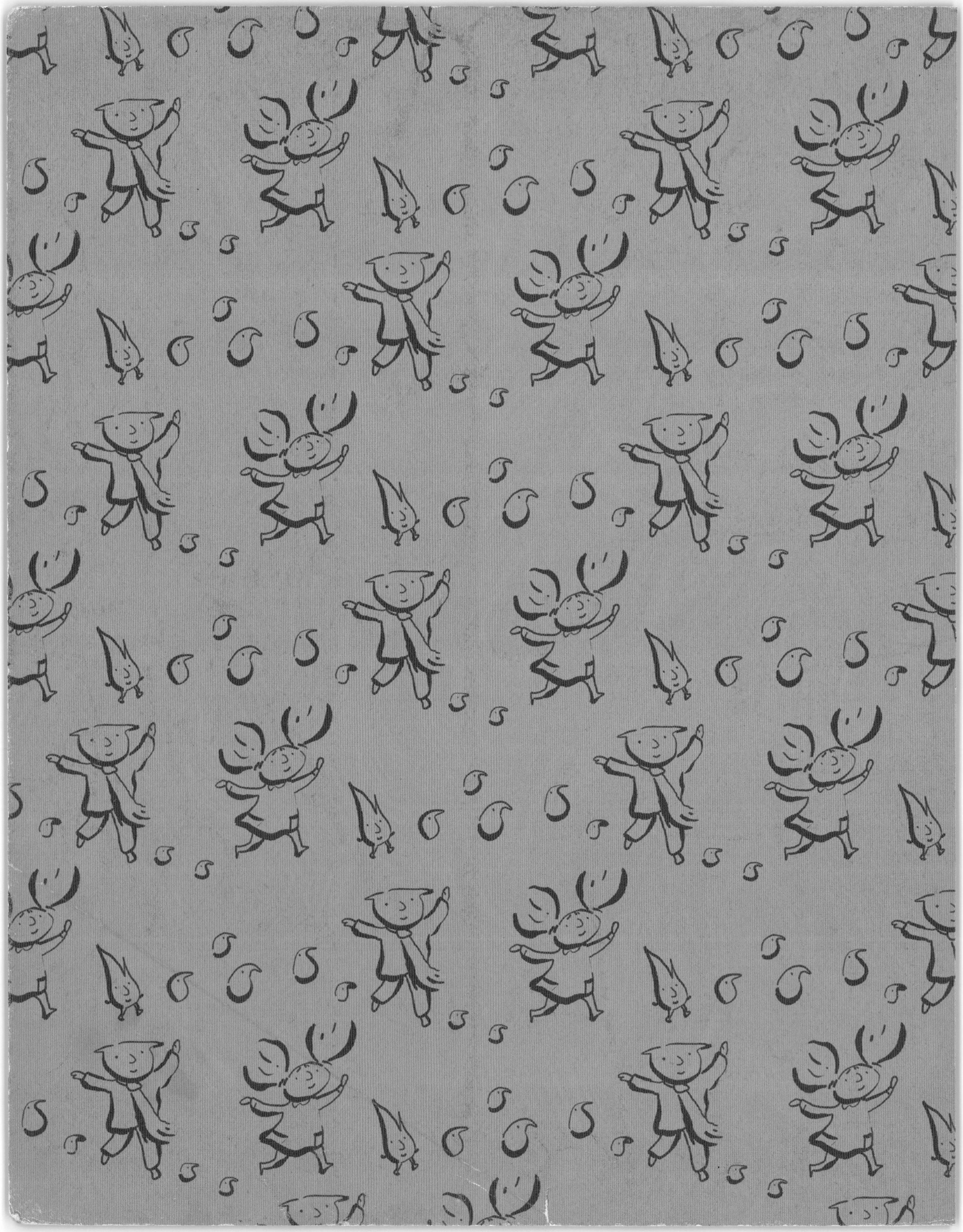

The Adventures of
ABNEY & TEAL
Other books from Abney and Teal:

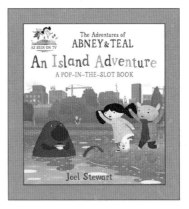

ISBN 978-1-4063-4421-9   ISBN 978-1-4063-4491-2

Abney and Teal toys also available:

**ABNEY & TEAL MIX &
MATCH CARD GAME**

ABNEY & TEAL BEAN TOY ASSORTMENT

**ABNEY & TEAL 24 PIECE
FLOOR PUZZLE**

ABNEY RAG DOLL

TEAL RAG DOLL